The History of the Kansas City Royals

by Richard Rambeck

MG (4-8)
ATOS 6.7
1.0 pts
Non-Fiction

25996 EN

DATE DUE

KANSAS CITY

RICHARD RAMBECK

THE HISTORY OF THE

ROYALS

CREATIVE EDUCATION

Published by Creative Education
123 South Broad Street, Mankato, Minnesota 56001
Creative Education is an imprint of The Creative Company

Designed by Rita Marshall
Editorial assistance by Tracey Cramer and John Nichols

Photos by: Allsport Photography, AP/Wide World, Focus on Sports,
Fotosport, SportsChrome.

Library of Congress Cataloging-in-Publication Data

Rambeck, Richard.
The History of the Kansas City Royals / by Richard Rambeck.
p. cm. — (Baseball)
Summary: Highlights the key personalities and memorable games in the
history of the team, begun in 1969, whose wealthy owner, Ewing Kauffman,
vowed to make the Royals into champions.
ISBN: 0-88682-911-9

1. Kansas City Royals (Baseball team)—History—Juvenile literature.
[1. Kansas City Royals (Baseball team)—History. 2. Baseball—History.]
I. Title. II. Series: Baseball (Mankato, Minn.)

GV875.K3R355   1999
796.357'64'09778411—dc21   97-7132

First edition

9 8 7 6 5 4 3 2

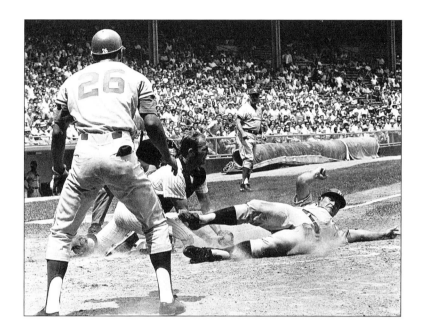

Located nearly in the center of the United States, Kansas City is a major hub of rail transportation, commerce, and industry in the Midwest. The second-largest city in Missouri, it is located on the Missouri–Kansas border, where it overlooks the Missouri River.

Kansas City, a thriving metropolis with nearly 450,000 people, is home to 13 colleges and universities, an unusually high number for a city of its size. The city also has a rich sports tradition, due to the Kansas City Chiefs of the National Football League and to a baseball team that has been one of the best in the major leagues during the past three decades.

Outfielder/catcher Ed Kirkpatrick.

Led by manager Joe Gordon, the Royals won 69 games and finished in fourth place.

The Kansas City Royals, formed in 1969 as an expansion team in the American League, enjoyed tremendous early success, winning six division titles, two American League pennants, and one World Series championship in a little more than 20 years. The stars of '70s and '80s like George Brett and Frank White set an incredibly high standard that the Royals of the 1990s have yet to match. But the team appears to be on the rise. Budding stars like Johnny Damon, along with veterans like Kevin Appier and Jeff King, hope to make their own mark in the team's glorious history.

KAUFFMAN'S ACADEMY PRODUCES SUCCESS

The Royals' quick rise as a contender in the American League can be attributed mostly to one man: team owner Ewing Kauffman. "Mr. K," as the fans called him, spent $6 million to assume ownership of the Royals, but that was only his initial expense. Kauffman decided he would spend whatever it took to build the best minor-league system in baseball. He was convinced that was the only way for the Royals to succeed as an expansion team. His logic proved correct. The key to the Royals' success in developing quality young talent was the Kansas City Royals Baseball Academy, a kind of school for young players. Other major-league owners laughed at Kauffman's idea—at first. But the Baseball Academy would soon produce amazing results.

The idea was to find 30 of America's finest natural athletes—not necessarily baseball players—and teach them to play the game. The concept worked; in no time at all, the unique academy's first graduating class was dominating

Steady slugger Jeff King.

other minor-league teams. Although the academy eventually closed, it helped produce one of the finest minor-league systems in baseball. It also laid the foundation for the Royals' success throughout the 1970s and into the 1980s.

The amazing Royals posted their first winning season (85–76) in 1971, which was only the third year of the team's existence. Kansas City, behind the talents of outfielders Amos Otis and Lou Piniella, wound up second in the American League West Division, finishing behind the powerful Oakland A's. Unfortunately for the Royals, they were doomed to wind up behind the A's for the next five years. Oakland, a franchise that had once called Kansas City home, won five consecutive AL West titles from 1971 through 1975. Although the Royals' early efforts were overshadowed by the powerhouse A's, K.C. fans kept the faith. The team's young players were just rounding into form, and one in particular was beginning what would be an amazing career.

1 9 7 1

On July 9, shortstop Fred Patek became the first Royal to hit for the cycle.

ROYALS A HIT, BY GEORGE

By the mid-1970s, the Royals had built a team of impressive talent: outfielder Amos Otis, first baseman John Mayberry, infielder Hal McRae, second baseman Frank White, and pitchers Dennis Leonard and Steve Busby made Kansas City a team to be reckoned with. The undisputed leader of the ballclub, however, was a burly third baseman named George Brett. The 22-year-old Brett batted .308 in 1975, which was only his second full season in the big leagues. He also led the American League in hits (195) and triples (13) that season. As his teammates and the rest of the league would soon discover, Brett would only get better.

Brett, a fun-loving sort, didn't let the pressure get to him. "George loves the game; it's that simple," said pitcher Andy Hassler, a longtime friend of Brett's. "He's out there to have fun. That eases a lot of the pressure. The best thing about him is that he doesn't take himself too seriously, not like a lot of superstars."

Brett may not have taken himself seriously, but opponents wondered if he was seriously strange. Opposing catchers claimed Brett talked to himself constantly while he was at the plate. "Sometimes I think the catcher can hear me, but I try not to let him," Brett said. "I'll say, 'I'm hot,' or 'I'm really swinging the bat good,' or 'I'm going to hit this pitcher.' But, hey, that's where it ends. It's not like I'm always having conversations with myself. I mean, I don't go back to my hotel room and say, 'What do you want to watch on TV, George? Oh, I don't know. Johnny Carson looks pretty good tonight.'"

It was Brett and the Royals who looked pretty good in 1976. Led by second-year manager Whitey Herzog, the Royals finally aced out the A's and won the American League West title with a 90–72 record. Brett won the American League batting title with a .333 average. He also had 215 hits and 14 triples. McRae wound up second in the league in hitting, just one-thousandth of a point behind teammate Brett. In addition, Kansas City's pitching staff, led by Doug Bird, Paul Splittorff, Larry Gura, and Busby, was one of the best in the American League.

In the American League Championship Series, the Royals fell behind the New York Yankees two games to one. Facing

1 9 7 6

Whitey Herzog was named the AL Manager of the Year for leading the Royals to the division crown.

Mark Gubicza, an exacting pitcher.

The competitive Frank White.

elimination in game four of the best-of-five series at fabled Yankee Stadium in New York, Kansas City scored three runs in the fifth inning to claim a 7–4 victory. In game five the Royals fell behind 6–3, but Brett's home run keyed a three-run eighth-inning rally to tie the game. In the bottom of the ninth, however, New York first baseman Chris Chambliss hit a lead-off home run to give the Yankees the victory.

New York had the American League pennant, but the Royals had high hopes for the future. They lived up to most of those hopes by winning division titles in 1977 and 1978. But Kansas City came up short each year in the American League Championship Series against the New York Yankees.

1 9 7 7

Hal McRae socked 54 doubles—good enough to lead the AL and also set a Royals record.

WILSON IS K.C.'S RUNNING MAN

Even though the 1978 season ended in disappointment for the Royals, the future was brightened by the emergence of a new star, a fleet-footed outfielder named Willie Wilson. Wilson was the type of player that the Royals Baseball Academy once produced.

He was a great athlete—one of the fastest humans alive, in fact—but not necessarily a great baseball player. "Wilson may be the fastest person I've seen in a uniform," manager Whitey Herzog claimed. "The whole thing with him is his bat. If he develops, he could be an awesome player."

Wilson, however, took awhile to develop, mainly because the Royals insisted the right-handed hitter learn to switch-hit. "They called me up in '77 after winter ball in Puerto Rico, where I did terrible," Wilson recalled. "They said, 'We're gonna make you a switch-hitter.' It was pretty tough for me

12

to turn around and hit a baseball from the other side at the age of 22. That's something kids do when they're eight and nine years old. I disagreed with it at first, but they said, 'If you want to get to the majors, this is the best way to do it.'"

Actually, the Royals told Wilson he would never be a major-leaguer unless he either switch-hit or batted left-handed only. "Now I'm glad they asked me to do it," Wilson said. "Otherwise, I don't think I'd have made it to the majors this quickly."

But Wilson struggled during the 1978 season, hitting only around .200. "I thought he'd chosen the wrong sport," said Brett, who watched in horror as Wilson swung wildly at pitches that were nowhere near the strike zone. "He was down on himself. He needed encouragement, confidence, and a lot of instruction." The Royals, however, were willing to give Wilson time to learn how to be a switch-hitter, especially because he could steal a base or two every time he got on. "When I get to first," Wilson said, "I figure second and third will be mine in just a second or two."

Kansas City also loved Wilson's speed in the field. "He's just got an average arm, but I don't think anybody in the American League can go as far on a fly ball and catch it," said Jim Frey, who took over for Whitey Herzog in 1979 as Kansas City's manager.

Wilson improved dramatically in 1979, but the Royals dropped to second in the AL West behind the surprising California Angels. Frey's first year as the Royals' manager was filled with injuries and disappointments. George Brett had a remarkable year—23 home runs and 107 runs batted in—but he also missed several key games with aches and pains that

1 9 7 9

Center fielder Amos Otis established a club record with 10 putouts in a game against Texas.

13

resulted from surgery before the season. Infielder Hal McRae also missed some games because of off-season surgery.

The Royals, however, put it all together in 1980. Pitcher Dennis Leonard won 20 games, and Larry Gura added 18 victories. Wilson hit .326, and John Wathan batted .305 while splitting time between catching and playing the outfield and first base. Meanwhile, regular first baseman Willie Mays Aikens smacked 20 home runs and drove in 98 runs. But nobody in baseball had a better year in 1980 than Brett. He hit .390, the highest batting average in the majors since Boston Red Sox star Ted Williams posted a .406 mark in 1941.

Brett actually didn't start the 1980 season very well, hitting only .247 in the middle of May. But he was a notoriously slow starter at the plate. By July, he had raised his average to .337. Then he really got hot. For the rest of the season, he batted .421. From July 18 to August 18, he put together a 30-game hitting streak. On August 17, his average jumped to more than .400 for the first time. Nine days later, Brett was batting .407, and he was hitting above .400 as late as September 19. He did all this in spite of missing 44 games because of injuries.

"We all come here with talent," McRae said. "But the stars are the ones who don't have to work at concentrating. The superstars are the ones who are unconscious. They're in a trance. That's what George was in. I've been there, too, but not for as long. You can actually visualize the line drive jumping off your bat when you're still kneeling in the on-deck circle."

Behind Brett's outstanding play, the Royals jumped back to the top of the AL West. They won their fourth division title in

1 9 8 2

Closer Dan Quisenberry saved 35 games to lead the AL—one of five times in his career.

Powerful outfielder Bo Jackson.

The incomparable George Brett.

five years and then faced the New York Yankees in the American League Championship Series. This time Kansas City would not be denied the pennant. The Royals won the first two games in Kansas City, and then trailed 2–1 in the seventh inning of game three. After a double by Wilson and an infield single by shortstop U. L. Washington, Brett stepped to the plate to face New York ace relief pitcher Rich "Goose" Gossage. Brett looked out at Gossage and began talking to himself. "You're hot," he told himself. "This guy can't get you out."

Gossage didn't; Brett slammed his first pitch into the third tier of seats beyond the right-field fence. The Royals had a 4–2 lead, and their ace reliever, Dan Quisenberry, closed the door on the Yankees, giving Kansas City a three-game sweep and a spot in the World Series for the first time in franchise history.

In the World Series, the Royals split the first four games with the Philadelphia Phillies and had a 3–2 lead in the ninth inning of game five. But the Phillies, behind series Most Valuable Player Mike Schmidt, rallied for a 4–3 victory. The teams headed back to Philadelphia with the Royals just one game from elimination. Philadelphia, sensing the kill, scored two runs in the third inning and never gave up the lead, winning 4–1.

After winning the American League pennant in 1980, the Kansas City franchise underwent a lot of turmoil in the next few years. First, Dick Howser replaced Frey as manager midway through the 1981 season. The following year, the experts picked the aging Royals to finish fourth, which was lower in the standings than Kansas City had been in a long time. But the Royals' veterans responded. McRae wound up

1 9 8 3

George Brett hit three home runs and a single against Detroit, setting a team record for total bases (13) in one game.

The lightning-quick Willie Wilson (pages 18-19).   17

1 9 8 4

First baseman/DH Steve Balboni launched 28 home runs to lead the Royals for the season.

leading the league in RBIs with 133. Wilson won the American League batting title with a .332 average and also topped the league in triples with 15.

Additionally, Quisenberry outdistanced all American League relief pitchers with 35 saves. The Royals finished second in the division to the California Angels, which was considered excellent for a team that was thought to be over the hill. In 1983, however, the news would not be so good.

Midway through the 1983 season, four Royals—including longtime stars Wilson and Aikens—were arrested on drug charges. For weeks, sports headlines told of turmoil and court dates, not victory and teamwork. The Royals' season—and their sense of family—was ruined. Howser faced having to rebuild not only the team's aging pitching staff, but the club's morale as well. Amazingly, the Royals managed to accomplish both with one approach: giving expanded roles to young players, particularly pitcher Bret Saberhagen.

SABERHAGEN SPARKS THE ROYALS TO NEW HEIGHTS

The Royals, an exciting combination of young and veteran players, surprised everyone by winning the AL West title in 1984. Although they were swept in the American League Championship Series by Detroit, Kansas City players knew they had had a remarkable year.

The next season was even more remarkable. The main difference in 1985 was the performance of Bret Saberhagen, who was only 21 years old but pitched like a seasoned veteran. Saberhagen led a late-season comeback that gave the Royals the division title. He posted a 20–6 record and was honored with the American League Cy Young Award. Kansas City engineered another comeback in the American League Championship Series against Toronto. The Royals fell behind three games to one, but then rallied to win three straight and claim their second American League pennant.

The experts gave the Royals no chance of defeating cross-state rival St. Louis in the World Series. The Cardinals, after all, had won 101 games, the most in major league baseball. No one was really surprised when St. Louis won the first two games in Kansas City to take a commanding lead. The Royals then fell behind three games to one, just as they had against Toronto, and were just one game from winding up second-best again. But this time it didn't happen. Kansas City won game five, and then staged a late rally to claim game six and to tie the series 3–3. Saberhagen was the starting pitcher in game seven. Despite his youth, Saberhagen had been Mr. Clutch all year, pitching superbly when the Royals truly needed a victory.

When he took the mound for the deciding game of the World Series, Saberhagen was nervous but confident. He was also nearly unhittable. "They couldn't catch up to his fastball," claimed Kansas City catcher Jim Sundberg. "He's like 'Catfish' Hunter—you have to get him in the first couple of innings, or you're not going to get him at all." The Cardinals didn't get him at all. Saberhagen threw a complete-game shutout as the Royals rolled to an 11–0 victory. As St. Louis meekly went down in the top of the ninth, the Kansas City veterans couldn't wait to celebrate their first world title. Many of them were even screaming at Saberhagen to hurry up and end it. "It wasn't just a matter of waiting all year for

1 9 8 7

Kevin Seitzer set a Royals record for games played by a rookie with 161.

21

Bret Saberhagen, a relentless pitcher.

this moment," Saberhagen said. "Some of those guys had been waiting for a championship for 12, 13 years. Hal McRae, Frank White—they wanted the last out to hurry up and get there."

When the last out did come, veterans such as George Brett, White, and Jim Sundberg raced to hug their youngest teammate and the World Series Most Valuable Player—Saberhagen. "I've never seen a better young pitcher," said St. Louis manager Whitey Herzog, the Royals' former skipper. "He's phenomenal. [New York Mets pitcher Dwight] Gooden is more overpowering, but when he gets behind 2–0 [in the count], Gooden's going to come at you with the fastball. This kid can surprise you. He got a couple of strikeouts on change-ups that I would never have thought possible for someone so young."

1 9 8 8

Bo Jackson became the first 25-25 player in Royals history, belting 25 homers and stealing 27 bases.

BO DOES BASEBALL

Due to Bret Saberhagen's performance, Kansas City finally had its championship. But in the years that followed, the Royals had to find a way to replace a lot of veteran players who were nearing the ends of their careers. The rebuilding process was hampered by injuries to George Brett and Saberhagen, who struggled to a 7–12 record in 1986. But Kansas City's youth movement got a major boost in 1986 when Bo Jackson, who had just won the Heisman Trophy, which is given to college football's best player, decided to play pro baseball instead of pro football. Although Jackson later elected to try pro football as a "hobby," he maintained that his first love was

baseball. It isn't hard to see why. At 6-foot-1 and 225 pounds, Jackson had the physique of a bodybuilder and the strength of a weightlifter. He didn't just hit the ball—he put it into orbit.

"Players from both teams watch when Bo takes batting practice," Saberhagen said. "There's always the feeling that you're going to see something you never saw before, and we don't want to miss it." Players throughout the American League were talking about Jackson, who made his major-league debut in 1986 and became a full-time starter in the outfield in 1987. "Bo and Jose Canseco are the two guys that everybody wants to watch," remarked Seattle Mariners catcher Scott Bradley. "When they get done [with batting practice], you go into the clubhouse and swap stories about balls they hit. It doesn't matter if we haven't played the Royals for two months—Bo still gets talked about. Everyone has to have a topper Bo story."

Jackson, a left fielder with a sprinter's speed, not only knew how to hit long balls, he also knew how to play the outfield. "No matter how fast we're running toward one another after a fly ball, he seems to know where I am at all times," said Willie Wilson, who played next to Jackson in center field. "Bo's the only outfielder with whom I've never had a collision—thank God. Bo is the only baseball player that you sense can do whatever he wants—and you can't wait to see him do it."

John Wathan, who took over as manager during the 1988 season, was amazed at Jackson's ability to make up almost instantaneously for what seemed like an error. "You define mistakes differently with Bo," Wathan said, "because a mistake to a normal player isn't a mistake to Bo. He can outrun and outthrow mistakes."

Jackson could also outpower just about every player in baseball. He finished the 1989 season with 32 homers and 105 RBIs. He also stole 26 bases. Yet, despite Jackson's heroics, the Royals were unable to recapture their glory days. The team had finished second in the AL West to the Oakland A's in 1989 and was picked by many experts to unseat the powerful A's in 1990. But the Royals collapsed. Saberhagen, who won the 1989 American League Cy Young Award, was haunted all season by injuries and poor run support. Meanwhile, another recent Cy Young winner, Mark Davis, who promised to be the relief pitcher the Royals so desperately needed early in the season, was haunted as well—by his own poor performance.

The early '90s were another turbulent time for the Royals. The team lost some of its best players, including Willie Wilson, Jackson, and pitcher Saberhagen to age, injury, and free agency. In addition, Wathan was replaced by new manager Hal McRae two months into the 1991 season. Once again the Royals struggled with a mixture of youthful newcomers and experienced veterans.

Furthermore, after team founder Ewing Kauffman died in 1993, the Royals' management spent less money on the team. But things started to turn around for the Royals that year. The defense was upgraded with the addition of shortstop Greg Gagne and second baseman Jose Lind. Leading run-producer Mike MacFarlane was finally back from a knee injury that occurred in 1991, and first baseman Wally Joyner's batting average went from .269 in 1992 to .311 in 1994.

1 9 9 1

Infielder Terry Shumpert drew a walk in six straight at-bats— a Royals record.

Swift outfielder Johnny Damon (pages 26-27).

At the end of the 1993 season, Brett retired, having played 20 years with the Kansas City Royals. His 3,154 hits, 317 homers, and .305 lifetime batting average should someday open the doors to baseball's Hall of Fame. Brett is eligible for induction after the 1998 season.

Perhaps the biggest reason for Kansas City's comeback in 1993 and '94 was the Royals' pitching staff. Much maligned early in the decade, the pitching had improved dramatically by 1994. The Royals' management helped the cause by signing talented star pitcher and Kansas City native David Cone to a free-agent contract. Ironically, Cone had played one season with the Royals in 1986 before being traded to the New York Mets, where he won the major-league strikeout crown three times. In Kansas City, he joined forces with ace pitcher Kevin Appier, Mark Gubicza, and relief pitcher Jeff Montgomery to form a fearsome staff.

The Royals rode their star pitchers to records of 84–78 in '93 and 64–51 in strike-shortened 1994, but a lack of offense kept Kansas City out of first place. "We're a good baseball team," explained McRae. "We're just not a great one." The Royals' front office had expected more, however, so McRae was fired and replaced by Bob Boone.

The 1995 and '96 seasons did not provide many thrills for Kansas City fans. The Royals posted their first-ever last-place finish in 1996 with a 75–86 record. And 1997 was even worse; Kansas City was stung by injuries, plagued by an anemic offense, and finished 67–94. In the wake of the team's worst season, the Royals may return to their roots. "The great Kansas City teams of the '70s and '80s were built from

1 9 9 3

Reliever Jeff Montgomery tied for the league lead with 45 saves and earned a spot on the AL All-Star team.

within," said new K.C. manager Tony Muser. "And that's what we're going to do again."

ROYALS GO BACK TO THE FUTURE

The Royals no longer have their academy to produce young stars, but the franchise has rededicated itself to building through its farm system. "We're a small-market team, and the economics of baseball say this is the only way we can get it done," noted general manager Herk Robinson. "I think the young guys we have will get us turned around."

If the Royals hope to return to their glory days, young players like outfielder Johnny Damon will have to lead the way. The fleet Damon has the rare combination of speed and hitting ability that reminds many Kansas City fans of former greats Willie Wilson and Amos Otis. "How fast Johnny develops will say a lot about how long it will take us to get back on top," said Muser. In addition to Damon, the Royals are looking for continued excellence from veterans Jeff King, Dean Palmer, and Kevin Appier.

First baseman King has been a rock-solid offensive contributor since arriving from the Pittsburgh Pirates. Acquired before the 1997 season, King gives the Royals a steady power source in the middle of the lineup. Kansas City hopes to get a few more years out of the veteran like his '97 campaign, in which he hit 28 homers and knocked in 112 runs.

Palmer, a late 1997-season acquisition from the Texas Rangers, gives the Royals some steady steam from the right side of the plate as well as a sure glove and strong arm at

1 9 9 6

Jose Offerman led the club in average (.303), runs (85), hits (170), doubles (33), triples (8), and walks (74).

Steady outfielder Hal Morris.

Power-threat third baseman Dean Palmer.

third base. "We're excited about what kind of numbers Dean can produce power-wise in our park," said a smiling Muser. "He's going to have lots of chances to drive in runs."

The hard-throwing Appier has been the ace of the staff since 1992. His intimidating combination of hard fastball, split-finger fastball, and wicked slider leaves American League batters dazed and confused.

"I thought he'd throw me the splitter, but he got me with the heat," commented a befuddled Mo Vaughn of the Boston Red Sox after facing Appier. "Then next time I struck out on the slider, and the last time he froze me with the splitter. I had no clue."

With Damon and Palmer providing the speed and enthusiasm, and King and Appier lending winning experience, Kansas City looks to get back on a winning track. The Royals have met with regal success in the past, and the future holds hope for a return to glory. It may not be long before this proud franchise reclaims its spot atop the American League.

1 9 9 8

With 196 strikeouts the previous season, Kevin Appier was looking to become the Royals' newest young star.